W9-BTS-507

GETAWAY

Adapted by K. T. Fulani
Based on the script by Doug Molitor
illustrated by Jesus Redondo

Simon Spotlight
New York London Toronto Sydney

Based on the TV series *Totally Spies!*™ created by Marathon Animation as seen on Cartoon Network®. Series created by Vincent Chalvon-Demersay and David Michel

SIMON SPOTLIGHT
An imprint of Simon & Schuster Children's Publishing Division
1230 Avenue of the Americas, New York, New York 10020
© 2005 MARATHON-MYSTERY ANIMATION Inc. *TOTALLY SPIES!* and all related logos, names, and distinctive likenesses are the exclusive property of MARATHON ANIMATION. All rights reserved.
Cartoon Network and logo are trademarks of and © Cartoon Network 2005.
All rights reserved, including the right of reproduction in whole or in part in any form.
SIMON SPOTLIGHT and colophon are registered trademarks of Simon & Schuster, Inc.
Manufactured in the United States of America
First Edition 10 9 8 7 6 5 4 3 2 1
ISBN 0-689-87701-3
Library of Congress Catalog Card Number 2004107462

MEET DEFEAT

The professor stood on the crater rim of the Hawaiian volcano. All around him, steam rose from the volcanic rocks as he carefully set up his video camera and pushed the record button.

"This is Professor John Payley," he said, speaking into the camera. "Diary entry: Thursday, 0800 hours."

On a nearby camp table the needle on a seismometer jumped, measuring the volcano's unusual behavior.

"I'm baffled," Payley said, still speaking to the camera. "Every vulcanologist considers this a dormant volcano. But if that's true, then why . . . ?"

Before he could finish his sentence, a low rumble shook the ground.

"What on earth?" Payley said, gasping.

Whoosh! A burst of flame shot up between the professor and his camera. When it died down, the professor was gone! Molten lava bubbled up from the crater floor, covering the spot where the professor had stood.

The next morning, in sunny California, a small glider plane drifted out of the clouds over Beverly Hills High. It spiraled down . . . down . . .

down . . .

Wham! The glider crashed into the branches of a tree. Its top popped off, and three teenage girls tumbled out. They landed headfirst in the bushes.

Clover stood up, brushing leaves from her bobbed blond hair and grumbling. "That was, like, the perfect end to our harshest mission yet." Clover and her friends, Sam and Alex, were t e e n a g e spies. When they weren't in school—or shopping, or at the beach–they were traveling around the globe, stopping totally wacko villains from destroying the world.

"For sure," Sam agreed. She blew a strand of long red hair out of her face. "After what we've been through, school will be a breeze!" As if school was *ever* hard for Sam, Clover thought. Sam was like a walking encyclopedia; she knew facts about everything.

"Good thing tomorrow night is the big dance!" Alex added, tucking her short brown hair behind her ears. "I *so* need to unwind!" If Sam was the team's encyclopedia, then Alex was its human disco. She loved to have fun!

Suddenly a shadow fell across the bushes. The spies looked up. It was super-brat Mandy, the spies' archenemy at Beverly Hills High. The evil masterminds of the world had *noth-*

ing on this girl. The friends groaned. Mandy was the *last* person they wanted to see right now. Or ever, for that matter.

"Don't kick back yet, girls," Mandy said smugly. "This afternoon is the track meet. And having you three on our team . . . makes me glad I'm not." Smirking, Mandy walked away.

"The track meet!" Sam cried, smacking her forehead. "We forgot!"

It turned out to be a track meet that none of them would *ever* forget. To start with, Sam took first in the one-hundred-meter hurdles—*face* first, that is.

"Oof!" she grunted, tripping over a hurdle and sprawling flat on the track.

Then in the pole-vaulting competition, Clover set a team record—for lamest launch ever.

"Ahhh!" she cried as she ran smack into the high bar. She tumbled backward and landed with a *thump* on the mat.

And in the relay race, the girls were ahead—until Alex left the baton behind.

"Ohhh," she groaned as she fumbled Sam's pass. When Alex bent down to pick the baton up, the other racers knocked her to the ground.

It was official: Sam, Clover, and Alex were the worst things to ever happen to the Beverly Hills High track team.

After the meet, the girls returned to the mansion. "Let's just relax," said Sam as they all slipped into the hot tub.

"Yeah, relax." Clover closed her eyes, letting the water swirl around her. It began to swirl faster . . . and faster. . . .

Suddenly the bottom of the hot tub dropped away! All the water rushed out, washing the spies down with it.

A MISSION TO RELAX

"Aaaah!" the girls screamed. They tumbled down a long, looping water slide and landed in a shallow pool.

The spies looked up dizzily. Their boss, Jerry, was standing over them. The wild ride had been another one of Jerry's transportation tricks. He always had creative—and unexpected—ways of getting the girls to WOOHP headquarters.

"Well!" Jerry boomed at the soggy spies. "I'm glad you could drop in, ladies."

"Like we had a choice?" Clover snapped.

Sam didn't like where this was headed. Jerry only called the spies to his headquarters when he needed to send them on a mission. "Jerry, tell me you are kidding," she pleaded. "I mean, we just got back from the most intense mission we ever had!"

"We are wiped! Trashed! Tweaked!" Clover

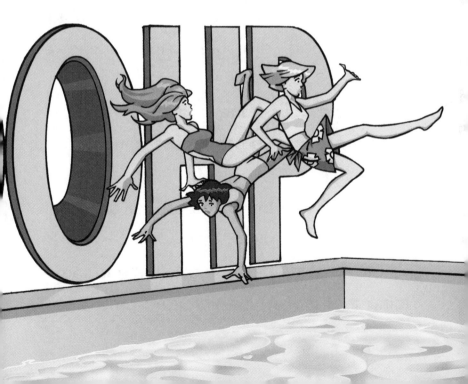

exclaimed, shaking her hair dry.

"Relax," Jerry said soothingly.

"How can we relax when you're about to send us on another mission?" Alex pointed out.

"A mission to relax," Jerry explained. "You're no asset to WOOHP when you're stressed, so I'm sending you on vacation. Here." He handed each of the girls a colorful beach bag. Sam pulled a turquoise towel out of hers.

"Let me guess," she said. "This is a bulletproof covering we use for escaping from a jungle prison?"

"No, this is a towel you use for drying off after a swim," Jerry replied.

Clover held up a tube of lotion and something that looked like a folded umbrella. "I bet this is a high-speed drill and a tube of blasting gel–to blow out a wall!" she guessed.

"No," Jerry said. "It's a beach umbrella and sunscreen, to prevent a sunburn. And before you ask, that's a nose clip for swimming," he added, pointing to the rubbery thing Alex had fished out of her bag. Alex smiled and swung the nose clip around like a lasso.

"Oh!" Jerry handed a small pink kit to Sam. "That's the Gadget Emergency Kit. A precaution. You won't need it."

"Let me get this straight," Sam said. "You're sending us somewhere to have *fun*?"

"How does Hawaii sound?" Jerry asked.

"Too good to be true," Clover said suspiciously.

"I have just one question," Sam said. "When does our flight leave?"

"In one minute. Just step in here," Jerry said. He led them over to a narrow doorway. The girls squeezed inside.

"This elevator's kind of small," Alex said.

"Does it take us right to our plane?" Sam asked.

"Oh, there's no plane," Jerry said. "A cruise missile is much faster. Bon voyage, ladies!"

Before the startled girls could say anything—*Ssshunk*! The door slid shut. Red warning lights flashed. The spies were

squashed together inside a guided missile.
And it was about to launch!

The girls hollered in protest. "Jerry!"

"I never fly by missile!"

"I'm totally claustrophobic!"

But Jerry just smiled and waved. With a
horrendous roar, the missile blasted off.

HAWAIIAN STYLIN'

Ssshunk! The missile door slid open. Sam, Clover, and Alex, still dressed in their swimsuits and clutching their beach bags, fell out and landed in a heap in the sand.

The spies sat up and looked around. White sand, blue water, swaying palm trees—could they really be in . . . *Hawaii*?

"Hiiiiiiii!" said a voice behind them.

Sam, Alex, and Clover jumped and spun around. A blonde woman with a big ponytail was standing behind them. "I'm Julie, your WOOHP travel agent!" she said in a game show-hostess voice. "You must be Sam, Clover, and Alex. I have your vacation all set!"

Sam scowled. The glare off Julie's big smile was practically blinding, she thought. "Julie, could you be not quite so perky?" she snapped. Julie's smile faded—but only for a second.

Alex looked at the towering waves—and the totally hot surfers riding them. "I can't believe it!" she squealed. "We're really in Hawaii! This is, like, my ultimate fantasy trip!"

"Up the beach we have hula dancing!" Julie said cheerfully.

"If it'll get you to dial down the perkiness, I'm there," muttered Sam. She hula danced away from the annoying travel agent.

"My kind of dance is the Taualunga," Alex said.

"Or you could just lie back and work on your tan!" Julie suggested.

"Now that's my kind of work," Clover replied, whipping out her towel.

"I want action!" Alex said, dancing the Taualunga around Clover. "Like tomorrow night . . . when we rock out to the finest band in Beverly Hills, Ultra Loud Zone!" She danced past a row of surfboards stuck in the sand.

Suddenly–*wham!*–a board almost flattened her. Alex leaped back.

"Sorry," someone said. "My board got away from me."

Alex looked up, and her eyes nearly popped out of her head. She was standing face-to-face with the cutest surfer *ever*! His hair was blond and shaggy, his eyes were "Surf's up!" blue, and his tan arms rippled with muscles. Alex stared at him.

"M-My name's Alex," she stuttered at last. "Who are you?"

"Corey," he replied. "I came here to study

volcanoes with my college professor, which is totally cool, 'cause Hawaii is my ultimate fantasy trip."

"Really? Mine too!" Alex squeaked. And this was her ultimate fantasy *guy*, she thought.

"Excellent!" Corey nodded. "Yeah, I love the food, the people, the music . . . though

I'm not much good at hula dancing."

"No?" asked Alex.

"My favorite dance is one you might never have heard of. It's called the Taua-lunga," Corey said.

Alex's jaw dropped. "Mine too!" she squealed. "This is almost, like, destiny! Who's your favorite band?"

Corey scratched his head. "Wow, that's tough. There's thousands to choose from. But I'd have to say my favorite is Ultra—"

"—Loud Zone!" Alex cried in unison with Corey. Her heart thudded like a Hawaiian drum. "You doing anything later?" she asked.

Corey glanced up at the quiet volcano in the center of the island. "No," he replied. "Yesterday Professor Payley was supposed to bring me up to his camp at that dormant volcano . . . but he never showed." He shrugged and smiled at Alex. "Wanna catch a wave?"

"Oh, sure! Surfin' is the only life for me," said Alex, who had never set foot on a surfboard in her life. She grabbed Corey's board and headed toward the water—but she stopped when she saw the waves. "Whoa! Right. Just gotta tell my friend where I'll be," she told Corey. Alex dashed over to Clover, who was still lying in the sun. "Clover, have you got a minute?" she asked.

Clover squinted up at her friend.

Alex grinned sheepishly and said, "I need you to teach me how to surf."

WAVE DAZE

"How big do these waves get?" Alex asked Corey, who was paddling next to her.

"Oh, three," Corey said casually. "Maybe four."

"Feet?" Alex smiled. This would be a cinch!

"Stories," Corey replied.

"Four stories?!" Okay, *now* Alex was worried. She gasped as the approaching wave rose forty feet in the air.

"Here I go!" Corey cried. He zipped

through the wave's curl and gracefully steered in to the beach. "Awesome!" he exclaimed. "C'mon, Alex!"

Alex gulped and paddled frantically. This guy was cute, but there was *no way* she was surfing down a skyscraper-size wave. "Corey, I have a confession!" she called back. "I've never surfed anything bigger than, uh, a thirty-five-foot wave!"

"Okay, hold on, Alex!" Corey shouted. But before he could set foot into the water— *Whoosh!* Flames burst from the ground around Corey. When the fire died down, there was nothing left but a charred patch of sand. Corey was gone!

SUSPICIOUS ACTIVITY

Alex stumbled onto shore as Sam and Clover ran up.

"He stood right there and vanished in a burst of fire. It was like a volcano erupting!" Alex screamed, out of breath from her fight with the colossal waves.

Clover reached down and inspected the charred circle in the sand. "This doesn't look like sand to me," she said.

"It's obsidian," Sam said, looking over

Clover's shoulder. "Volcanic glass."

"Is there *anything* you don't know?" Clover asked.

Suddenly Alex gasped. "Corey said his professor flaked out and never showed up for his field trip . . . to study that volcano!" She pointed at the tall mountain in the center of the island.

"I've got a bad feeling about this," Sam said. "I'm calling Jerry." She pulled a powder compact out of her swimsuit. When she flipped it open, a tiny screen appeared. The compact was actually a spy communicator! "Jerry, this is Sam," she said. "Hello?"

Jerry's face flashed onto the screen. But a second later the image fizzled.

"Forget it. Your Compowder got wet," Alex said. "We'll try ours." But their Compowders were soaked too.

"Maybe there's something in the kit we can use," Sam said, pulling the Gadget Emergency Kit out of her bag. Inside she found a laptop computer the size of an eye shadow case. She typed in "volcano," and a world map blinked onto the tiny screen.

"WOOHP has a volcano research lab in

Iceland," Sam said. "Maybe they can answer our questions."

Just then they heard what could only be described as one of the most annoying sounds known to mankind.

"Hiiiiiii!" said a perky voice. The girls cringed and whirled around. Julie was standing right behind them.

"Julie, we have to get to Iceland," Alex told the travel agent.

"No problem! I'll arrange it," Julie replied with a smile. She whipped out a remote control and hit a button.

THAT'S WHY THEY CALL IT ICELAND

At last the missile stopped over a glacier. *Ssshunk!* The door slid open. Still dressed in their swimsuits, the spies fell out onto an icy slope. They slid down and landed in a pile of snow.

The girls sat up, shivering. "This is so *cold*!" Alex cried.

Just then a man ran out of the research lab. He was wearing a heavy coat and a ski hat. "What are you doing in Iceland dressed

like this?" he asked the spies.

"C-Could we d-discuss this over a hot, grande, d-decaf soy latte?" Sam replied through chattering teeth.

Moments later the girls were dressed in robes and sipping hot coffee inside the research lab. Dr. Sorenson, the head of the lab, listened as they explained why they'd come.

"We need to know if you've had any reports of volcanic eruptions in Hawaii," Alex said.

Dr. Sorenson nodded and pointed to a map on the wall. Lights marked the locations of volcanoes all over the world. "We had one yesterday and one earlier today," he said. "Both were near a dormant volcano, so we assume they were false alarms. If there were eruptions, we'd have heard from our vulca-nologist there, Professor Payley."

"Professor Payley?" the spies cried in unison.

"He's been missing since yesterday," Alex explained. "And his mega-cute student, Corey, vanished earlier today!"

Before Dr. Sorenson could answer, an alarm horn blared. Suddenly all the lights on the map began to flash. "Now I *know* we have a bug in the system," Dr. Sorenson said.

"Are you sure the eruptions aren't real?" Sam asked.

"My dear," he replied smugly, "if all these volcanoes were to erupt at once, it would mean massive global destruction."

"So it's safe to go back to Hawaii?" Alex asked.

Dr. Sorenson frowned. "If people are disappearing there, I wouldn't call it *safe*. You're not thinking of going back?"

The spies looked at one another and smiled. That was *exactly* what they were thinking.

A BIG FALL

A short time later the spies parachuted down from the missile. They landed on the volcano crater's rim.

Alex began to stuff her parachute back into the tiny Gadget Emergency Kit. "How did they get these things *in* the kit?" she wondered aloud.

"Pass me the binocular shades," Sam said. Alex handed her a pair of stylish sunglasses with pink frames. When Sam put them on, the lenses telescoped into binoculars. She

peered down into the volcano.

"I don't see any sign of Payley," Clover said. "Can we go home now?"

"Wait a sec," Sam said. She zoomed in on a shiny object. "I see something down there. It looks like . . . glass!"

The girls carefully made their way down the rest of the slope. On the floor of the crater, Sam found the object she'd spotted through the binoculars: a pair of wire-rimmed glasses. "Forget the he-went-home theory," she said. "He wouldn't leave these."

"Look!" Clover exclaimed. "A camcorder!"

"Hey, let's make a video of us!" Alex said, reaching for the video camera.

"Don't!" Sam cried. "It may have recorded

a clue." She hit the rewind button. "Let's see what he was doing." She tapped PLAY.

A man with the same wire-rimmed glasses appeared on-screen. "What on earth . . . ?!" he cried. Suddenly he disappeared in a blaze of orange fire.

"There was an eruption!" Alex exclaimed. "And the Professor vanished just like Corey!"

"One problem, Alex," Clover said. She picked up a rough, black rock. "If this was all molten lava yesterday, how come the rocks look totally the same today?"

"Did you guys see this crack?" Clover said, pointing. The crack formed a wide circle in the crater floor. "Duh! It's so obvious it's a trap—doooorrrrr!" Suddenly the ground dropped out from under the spies. It was a trapdoor, all right. And they had fallen for it!

A SECRET HIDEOUT

The spies landed in a wide room. Video screens and control panels lit up the rock walls around them. They had stumbled into a high-tech hideout deep inside the volcano.

"Corey!" Alex exclaimed suddenly. The cute surfer and Professor Payley were locked in a cell in the corner of the room. Alex raced over to them. "You're all right!" she cried.

"Alex, get out of here before they catch you too!" Corey told her.

Just then the spies heard footsteps. Two men with laser guns appeared in the doorway. "Intruders!" they shouted.

"I'll be back for you, Corey!" Alex cried. Dodging laser blasts, Alex, Clover, and Sam dashed through a side tunnel.

The tunnel ended in a vast cavern. The spies skidded to a halt. They were standing on a narrow catwalk suspended over a massive lake of glowing lava.

"Whoa!" Clover cried. "We just hit volcano central!"

Sam pointed up at a huge laser hanging from the ceiling. Its red beam was aimed at a bubbling spot in the center of the lava lake.

"It looks like that humongous laser keeps the lava cooking," Alex said.

"I bet this place is wired in to every other volcano on earth!" Sam declared.

"What kind of freak came up with this?" Clover wondered.

"That would be me!" a voice growled behind them.

The girls whirled around and gasped. Standing at the end of the catwalk was a man in a hooded robe. On either side of him,

three henchmen in hooded robes pointed their lasers at the girls.

The man chuckled horribly. "Dr. Hefestus is the name, global devastation is my game," he said in a raspy voice. "Forgive me if I startled you."

"Meeting people is so awkward," Clover replied. "Let's try this again–from the *top*!"

At once the three spies charged the

villains. Swinging their beach bags, they knocked the lasers out of the henchmens' hands. The weapons tumbled into the molten lava below.

The girls dashed down a flight of stairs toward the laser control panel. They had to shut off that laser!

Suddenly a ring of flames blazed up from the floor around the spies, trapping them. Dr. Hefestus chuckled. "Careful, girls," he said. "Volcanic fire ruined my face . . . as it will *yours*." He pulled back his hood. The spies gasped. His face looked like it had been melted!

Hefestus grabbed a lever on the control panel. When he pulled it, lights began to blink all over a giant world map. "My machine can erupt every volcano on the earth," he told the spies. "When the world is covered in lava, you will all look like me! Ha-ha-ha-haaaa!" He cackled wildly.

"You have serious issues, Doc," Clover said. "Though I'm sure it's nothing a little facial wouldn't cure."

"You know, I can relate," Alex said. "That week I had a pimple . . . I was a major witch."

"True," Clover replied. "But we loved you anyway."

Sam scowled at them. "Hel-*lo*, we're saving the world here, remember?" she said.

Then she turned to the madman. "Your evil plan won't succeed, Hefestus. Not if we have anything to say about it!"

Suddenly the ring of fire disappeared. Hefestus's henchmen grabbed the girls. Within moments the spies were hanging by their ankles over the bubbling lava lake.

"I guess we don't have anything to say about it," Alex remarked. The girls looked down at the lava. Inch by inch they were being lowered closer . . . and closer. . . .

RED HOT BLUES

"We're almost in the lava!" Clover cried. "And this heat is trashing my hair!"

"We have to do something!" Sam told the other spies. "Molten lava is about to cover the world!"

"Not to mention our hair!" Clover pointed out.

"Alex," Sam said, "give me your nose clip."

Alex handed the rubber nose clip to Sam. Sam twirled it around and lassoed the control switch. With a yank, she flipped the switch.

The bar they were hanging from raised up away from the molten lava. The spies landed safely on the catwalk.

"You go, cowgirl!" Clover said.

"Seize them!" Hefestus cried to his henchmen.

"I knew he'd say that," Sam said. "Split up!"

Sam, Clover, and Alex each dashed down a different tunnel. Hefestus's h e n c h m e n chased them, firing their laser guns.

Sam ducked into a side room

filled with computers. As a henchman closed in on her, she whipped out her beach towel and spun around. When the henchman tried to grab her, she wrapped the towel tightly around his head. The henchman crashed into a computer console and fell to the ground.

Meanwhile Clover was running down a long tunnel. Suddenly a henchman appeared in front of her. Clover reached into her bag and grabbed the folded beach umbrella. When she pushed a button, the umbrella extended. Now it was as long as a pole-vaulting pole! Clover dug the tip of the umbrella into the ground and launched into the air.

Wham! She slammed feetfirst into the henchman, knocking him down. The umbrella opened, and Clover twirled gracefully to the ground. Clover smiled. If only she could have done *that* at the track meet, she thought.

Just then another henchman charged Clover. She cut back toward the main control room. As she passed Alex, she handed her the tube of sunblock—and this time Alex *didn't* fumble the pass. She spun around and squirted lotion onto the floor, just as the henchman charged up.

"Aaaah!" he yelled as he hit the slippery floor. He slid all the way into an empty cell. Alex slammed the door shut, locking him inside.

"Tell me where the keys are so I can let my friends out!" Alex demanded.

The henchman pulled the keys from his pocket and waved them at Alex. "I've got your keys right here . . . ," he taunted her.

Suddenly the keys were yanked from his hand. Alex had lassoed them with the nose clip! She ran over to Corey and the professor's cell and unlocked the door.

"Now help us trash that volcano machine!" she said to them.

Everyone ran toward the lava-filled cavern. To their horror, they saw that the lava lake was rising. It had almost reached the platform where they were standing! "We have to turn this off now!" Sam cried.

Clover hurled the beach umbrella like a javelin. When it hit, the laser control panel exploded in a burst of sparks. But it was no use. The lava was still rising!

"The lava's almost to our level!" Alex cried. As it oozed over the edge of the catwalk, the spies leaped onto the control panel.

"Hot-foot alert!" Clover yelled.

"Hey!" Alex said suddenly. She sniffed the air. "I smell garlic."

Garlic? Reaching down, Sam dipped her finger into the bubbling lava and tasted it. She gasped. "This is hot," she said. "As in *spicy*. But it's not lava—it's marinara sauce!"

"That's right, ladies," said a raspy voice.

"Hefestus!" Clover cried. The villain and his henchmen were wading toward them through the lava.

"There is no Hefestus," he rasped. He reached up and began to tug at his hideous face. Then it came off! Hefestus was really . . .

"Jerry?!" the girls cried in astonishment.

Hefestus's hooded henchmen peeled off their masks too. Underneath they were clean-cut, normal-looking spies. "And your henchmen are really WOOHP agents?" Sam said, suddenly understanding.

Alex turned to the cute surfer. "And Corey is really . . ." He pulled off his surfer mask. Underneath was a nerdy-looking guy with buckteeth and glasses. ". . . goofy," Alex finished.

The girls were totally confused. "We know you're not trying to destroy the world," Clover said to Jerry. "So what's going on?"

Just then a section of the crater floor opened and a monitor rose up, revealing Dr. Sorenson's face. "It was all part of the test," he told them.

"Everything was *fake*?" Sam exclaimed.

"Yes," Jerry said calmly. "This phony volcano was once a villain's hideout. Now I use it for our annual field test."

"You were *testing* us?" Clover said furiously.

"Did we pass?" Sam asked.

"Uh, no," Jerry said. "The lava got

you before you could save the world. So you all have to undergo retraining."

Alex turned to the goofy-looking boy. "Corey, you were in on this?" she asked.

"My name's not Corey," he replied in a nasal voice. "It's Morey."

Alex's heart sank.

Suddenly a loud rumble shook the cavern. The ground trembled beneath their feet. "What is this, Jerry?" Sam asked. "Extra credit?"

"No!" Jerry exclaimed as rocks began to crash down around them. "This is real!"

FULL OF HOT AIR

Alex groaned. "Great. We blow the track meet, I fall for a dork . . . and now this!"

"There is an actual volcano under your fake one," Dr. Sorenson cried from the monitor. "And it's erupting!"

With a crack the laser beam broke off from the ceiling and crashed down. The fake hideout was falling apart! Everyone ran toward an exit tunnel. The other WOOHP agents dashed outside. But before the spies,

Jerry, Morey, and Professor Payley could follow, a pile of rocks fell down, blocking the exit.

"They'll never be able to move all that stone in time!" Professor Payley cried. "We're trapped!"

A crack ripped across the rock floor, and molten lava bubbled up through it. But unlike Jerry's phony marinara lava, this lava had flames!

"Get back!" Jerry exclaimed. "That's real lava!"

Clover shrieked, "Look out!" Everyone jumped back as a giant chunk of rock crashed down from the ceiling. When the dust cleared, they could see a patch of blue sky overhead.

"If only we could fly through there!" Alex

said, pointing to the hole.

"That's it!" Sam exclaimed. "Alex, your parachute is in the Gadget Emergency Kit, right?"

"Yeah, but what can we do with it?" Alex asked.

"Make a hot air balloon," Sam replied, "if we can stretch the chute across the crack!" She pointed to the crack in the floor, w h e r e more fiery lava was oozing up.

"Leave it to me!" Clover exclaimed. She strapped on the parachute. Then she took a flying leap over the crack in the ground. Instantly the parachute inflated with hot air rising from the lava. Alex, Sam, Jerry, Morey, and Professor Payley grabbed on to Clover as the makeshift hot air balloon began to rise.

"Everybody hold on tight!" Sam cried.

Up, up, up they floated . . . until at last they were out of the volcano. And not a moment too soon! A second later the volcano erupted in a fiery explosion. Lava spewed down the side of the mountain.

As the parachute drifted safely over the ocean, Jerry sighed with relief. "We made it, thanks to you girls. You showed real

resourcefulness!" he told the spies.

"Are you still going to flunk us?" Sam asked.

"No, you pass," Jerry replied, "with flying colors."

The spies grinned.

A REAL BLAST

"I've heard of guys being two-faced, but Morey was ridiculous," Alex said the next night as she, Sam, and Clover walked up to the Beverly Hills High cafeteria. Dressed in their sleekest outfits, the girls were headed for the school dance.

"Let's forget Hawaii and just enjoy the dance," Sam said as she opened the door. "I wonder what theme they picked."

The girls stopped in their tracks and

stared. The whole cafeteria was decorated with fake palm trees. Students in grass skirts and flower leis hula danced past them. And right in the center of the room was a huge

papier mâché volcano. Suddenly the volcano opened and Mandy, who was head of the decorating committee, popped out.

"No! Not that! Anything but that!" the spies cried. They had had enough volcanoes for one week. Turning on their heels, they raced out of the cafeteria, slamming the doors behind them.

Mandy saw them leave and rolled her eyes. "They *seriously* need to get a life," she said.